HOPSCOTCH
TWISTY TALES

The
Three Frilly
Goats Fluff

By Adam and Charlotte Gillain
and Phil Littler

W
FRANKLIN WATTS
LONDON•SYDNEY

This story is based on the traditional fairy tale,
The Three Billy Goats Gruff, but with a new twist.
You can read the original story in
Hopscotch Fairy Tales. Can you make
up your own twist for the story?

First published in 2012 by
Franklin Watts
338 Euston Road
London
NW1 3BH

Franklin Watts Australia
Level 17/207 Kent Street
Sydney
NSW 2000

Text © Adam and Charlotte Guillain 2012
Illustrations © Phil Littler 2012

A CIP catalogue record for this book is available
from the British Library.
ISBN 978 1 4451 0671 7 (hbk)
ISBN 978 1 4451 0677 9 (pbk)

Series Editor: Melanie Palmer
Series Advisor: Catherine Glavina
Series Designer: Peter Scoulding

Printed in China

Franklin Watts is a division of
Hachette Children's Books,
an Hachette UK company
www.hachette.co.uk

Once upon a time there were
three Frilly Goats Fluff.

The three Frilly Goats Fluff wore frilly hats.

They wore frilly jumpers.

They wore frilly pants.

In fact EVERYTHING they wore looked frilly (and silly)!

The three Frilly Goats Fluff longed to go to the shops to buy more frilly things.

But there was a problem. A very big problem: the Troll.

The Troll lived under the bridge.

He was rough. He was tough.

He did all kinds of Troll-like stuff.

Especially eating goats

who crossed his bridge!

One day, the small Frilly Goat Fluff thought, "This scarf doesn't go with my top. I'm going to the shops."

She was scared of the Troll, but she really wanted a new scarf, so off she went.

"Who's that trip-trap-trapping over my bridge?" roared the Troll.

12

"Here, wear this!" bleated the small Frilly Goat Fluff. "You would look really nice in it." She threw her old scarf at the Troll.

The middle-sized Frilly Goat Fluff was trying on her old earrings. "These earrings are far too big for me," she sighed. "I need new ones."

She was scared of the Troll,
but she really wanted a new
pair of earrings, so off she went.

"Who's that trip-trap-trapping over my bridge?" roared the Troll. "Here, wear these!" bleated the middle-sized Frilly Goat Fluff. "They would look great with your scarf."

The middle-sized Frilly Goat Fluff
threw her earrings at the Troll.

The big Frilly Goat Fluff looked at her handbag. "This bag doesn't go with anything," she grumbled. "I'm going to the shops."

She was scared of the Troll, but she really wanted a new bag, so off she went.

"Who's that trip-trap-trapping over my bridge?" roared the Troll.

"Here, take this bag!" bleated the big Frilly Goat Fluff. "The colour matches your outfit." The big Frilly Goat Fluff threw her bag at the Troll.

The three Frilly Goats Fluff had
a great time at the shops.

Under the bridge, the Troll tried on all his new things.

"I like looking frilly," he said to himself. "I want more frilly things."

The three Frilly Goats Fluff finished
shopping and walked home.
When they got to the bridge,
the Troll was waiting ...

… to show off his new clothes!

"You look great!" the three Frilly Goats Fluff said. "From now on, we'll all go shopping together!"

Puzzle 1

Put these pictures in the correct order.
Which event do you think is most important?
Now try writing the story in your own words!

Puzzle 2

1. I love scaring everyone.

2. We change our clothes a lot.

3. We love going shopping.

4. I'm too tough to wear frilly things.

5. I ate goat stew for dinner.

6. Fashion is very important.

Choose the correct speech bubbles for each character. Can you think of any others? Turn over to find the answers.

Answers

Puzzle 1

The correct order is: 1a, 2f, 3e, 4b, 5d, 6c

Puzzle 2

The Troll: 1, 4, 5

The three Frilly Goats Fluff: 2, 3, 6